LAST LOOK FROM THE MOUNTAIN

Published by Raintree Publishers Inc., 205 West Highland Avenue, Milwaukee, Wisconsin 53203.

Art Direction: Su Lund

Printed in the United States of America.   1 2 3 4 5 6 7 8 9 0 87 86 85 84 83

Library of Congress Cataloging in Publication Data
Marron, Carol A.   Last look from the mountain.   "A Carnival Press book."
Summary: Kirsten spends a final summer with her grandmother in the mountains of Norway, helping her to care for her herd of sheep. [1. Norway—Fiction. 2. Grandmothers—Fiction. 3. Shepherds—Fiction]
I. Ray, Deborah, ill.   II. Title.
PZ7.M349Las   1983   [Fic]   83-6450   ISBN 0-940742-17-9

LAST LOOK
FROM THE
MOUNTAIN

Story by Carol A. Marron

Illustrations by Deborah Kogan Ray

A Carnival Press Book Raintree Publishers Inc.

Father grew up on the old farm. Now he's a fisherman, and we live by the sea. Every summer he's taken me fishing.

I think I love the blue meadow almost as much as he does.

We have always been close to each other, and this year I discovered some new things about Father.

APRIL

When Grandmother called, Father had to leave his boat and drive to the old farm. For some strange reason, Norwegian lambs like being born at night.

"You're big enough to help now, Kirsten," he told me. "Next year the sheep will be Cousin Erik's problem."

7

It was cold in the shed. I shivered when Father took the skin from a dead lamb and tied it over an orphaned one.

"So the dead one's mother will think this little one is hers," Grandmother explained.

I patted the suspicious ewe. "Here," I told her. "It smells like your baby, doesn't it?" Finally she let the lamb nurse.

"You have a new mother now," I whispered to the baby.

We ate herring for breakfast the next morning. I knew they reminded Father that he should have been fishing.

"I can't keep leaving my boat, and you can't live here at the gård alone," he told Grandmother. "In the spring you must sell the winter farm to Erik and come stay with us."

"We'll see, Arild." Grandmother folded her hands and said nothing more.

June

Grandmother insisted on taking the sheep to her mountain hut for one last summer. Father insisted I stay there too—to watch over Grandmother.

"Nobody herds sheep from a seter anymore," I argued. "Father, you promised to take me fishing this summer. I don't belong on a mountain and besides, I'm afraid of this old bull."

Father laughed and shook his head. "Old Soupbone is Grandmother's pet," he said. "He likes to stamp and snort, but that's only an act. I think you'll learn lots of things while you're here."

All I could think about at dinner was not being on the boat with Father.

Before going to bed that night, Grandmother left a bowl of porridge on the front steps. "It's for the elves," she said. "For good luck."

I wanted to run away, but all night I imagined little people surrounding the hut.

JULY

The sheep roamed free most of the time. Every few days Grandmother sent me out to count them. I did it as quickly as possible so I could run off and explore the mountain or swim in Grandmother's lake.

Evenings were usually quiet. I liked looking at the books in the seter, even though they smelled like damp cellars. Most of them belonged to Grandmother, but I found a few with Father's name on them.

"Grandmother," I asked, "why did Father leave the farm?"

Grandmother gazed over the valley in the same way Father looks at the ocean. "Arild suddenly wanted to be a sailor," she said. "Perhaps the mountain trolls told your father something that made him leave."

August

I was beginning to know Grandmother's sheep. The ewes always gossiped in the same little bunches of twos and threes. The same lambs chased the wind together, and I could easily find the lamb that had become my favorite.

I liked picking berries with Grandmother, but we had to sneak away from the sheep. If they saw our pails, they would follow us and beg.

One afternoon, we were in a patch of cloudberries when I saw a curious pile of rocks. It looked like a troll with a stony head. One arm pointed up the hillside. What was the troll trying to show me?

When Grandmother returned to the seter, I didn't go with her. The troll was telling me to climb the mountain.

It was a steep slope. When I reached a plateau, my legs were wobbly and I was breathing hard.

I sat down to rest, and there in the distance was Father's blue meadow, stretching out as far as I could see.

So this was the troll's secret! This was the reason Father left the mountain.

SEPTEMBER

One night a cold wind blew in from the sea. When we woke, the sheep were huddled outside the hut. "They think winter's come," Grandmother said with a sigh. "They're ready to go down the mountain, and I am too."

It took all day to walk the sheep and old Soupbone back to the gård. Summer herding had come to an end.

Father came to take us home, and
Cousin Erik waved to us as we drove away.
Grandmother didn't watch. She stared straight ahead.

"Don't worry, Grandmother," I whispered.
"We'll make Father take us back to the hut for
holidays."

Grandmother smiled then, just a little.

"You helped me learn to love the mountain,"
I told her. "Maybe Father and I can teach you to
love the sea."

Kirsten lives in *Norway,* a country once completely covered by glaciers. The ice fields carved long, narrow inlets, called *fjords,* into the land. Some fjords reach over one hundred miles inland and provide access for fishing boats and steamships. Deep mountain lakes and rivers were also formed by the glaciers.

Although only a little over three percent of the land is suitable for producing crops, there are many small farms (*gårds*) tucked among the hills and valleys of Norway. The mountain huts owned by farmers were once used for shelter when sheep and cows were taken to graze in summer pastures. Now these *seters* are used as cabins for country holidays.

Trolls and elves are popular characters in Norwegian legends. It is said that the many unusual rock formations scattered about the countryside were trolls before the sunlight turned them to stone. Today the image of these creatures is a common one, found on signposts, cards and many objects of art.

Carol Marron is the author of several books for young readers. She was born in Minneapolis, Minnesota, and still lives there with her husband and three children. The author dedicates this book "to Norma G."

Deborah Kogan Ray was born in Philadelphia and attended the Philadelphia College of Art, the Pennsylvania Academy of the Fine Arts, the Albert C. Barnes Foundation, and the University of Pennsylvania. She has had numerous solo and group shows and has received a Louis Comfort Tiffany Foundation Grant.

Ms. Ray has illustrated fifteen books for children, including *I Have a Sister, My Sister Is Deaf, That Is That, Through Grandpa's Eyes,* and *Sunday Morning We Went to the Zoo,* which she both wrote and illustrated. The artist dedicates this book "to Todd."

DATE DUE		
9-24-84 1527		MAY 0 2 1995
11-24-84 1529		SEP 1 0 1995
Mar 20 85		
JUL 25 1990		
AUG 16 1990		
FEB 28 1991		
FEB 18 93		
JAN 04 1994		
FEB 1 5 1994		
AUG 0 9 1994		
AUG 27 1994		
FEB 1 4 1995		

a-2-85
C.4-88 Atl 8-96 16-392